MYSTERY OF

THE ARK

MYSTERY OF
THE ARK

The Dangerous Journey to Mount Ararat

PAUL THOMSEN

INSTITUTE FOR CREATION RESEARCH
SANTEE, CALIFORNIA

Unless otherwise noted, all Scripture quotations are from the New King James Version of the Bible, © 1979, 1980, 1982, 1984 by Thomas Nelson, Inc., Nashville, Tennessee and are used by permission.

Illustrations by Brian Thompson

Institute for Creation Research
P.O. Box 2667
El Cajon, California 92021
619/448-0900 • www.icr.org

Library of Congress Cataloging-in-Publication Data

Thomsen, Paul M., 1938–
    Mystery of the ark: the treacherous ascent of Mt. Ararat/Paul
    Thomsen.—2nd ed.
        p. cm.—(Creation adventure series)
    Summary: Two teams of scientists search for Noah's Ark and
    experience instances of God's grace.
    ISBN 0-932766-46-3
    [1. Noah's ark—Fiction. 2. Ararat, Mount (Turkey)—
    Fiction. 3. Christian life—Fiction.] I. Title.
PZ7.T37375My 1991
[Fic]—dc20   97-070392
                                                                   CIP
                                                                   AC

To our kids,
all seven of them!

CHAPTER 1

"That's Yerevan, stay close to mountain," shouted Yavuz above the roar of the helicopter's big blades and jet engine.

Shaking his head, the American pilot pointed a gloved hand to the intercom mike and lifted his headset to an ear. Even then, the icy wind screaming through the doorless helicopter made his Turkish copilot barely audible. Pointing down from an altitude of eight thousand feet,the Turk yelled into his mike, "That's Russia—two miles to the right out there and we get shot down!" He made a hand-spinning motion with his gloved finger imitating a falling helicopter hit by a ground-to-air missile.

Nodding grimly, Chuck closed the gap to fifty meters with the snow-covered mountain on their left, sending the helicopter's shadow into a 160-knot dance across the crags and crevasses marring the north face. Ahead loomed the huge Ahora Gorge, nearly splitting the mountain in two. Like a wound from a giant dagger, it sliced the high glacier, then descended, leaving an ugly black scar stretching to the rugged, boulder-strewn foothills. At the base of the gorge, desert sands surrounded and held captive the largest landmass mountain in the world, seventeen-thousand-foot Mount Ararat.

Motioning his expedition mate in the rear seat to lean forward, American adventurer-explorer Chuck Aaron yelled, "This part of the world is filled with danger. Down there, down through the chin bubble, is the red-hot border of Iran, Russia, and Turkey. Out there," nodding out the open door to his right, "back over your shoulder, that's the border with Iraq. It's studded with missiles and lined with tanks. Over there, in those rugged foothills, that's where the Kurds live."

"The who?" shouted Bob.

"The Kurds—they're nomads living in tents. They don't recognize any borders—just follow their sheep and goats around. They're the ancient descendants of the mountain; they're not afraid of nothin' or nobody. Their forebears beat up on Genghis Khan and his Mongol hordes when they came through. Over there, way down by those crags and caves in the gorge, that's where the bandits from Russia and Iraq hide out. Back there," throwing his thumb toward the rear of the chopper, "that's where drug runners and terrorists infiltrate from Iran, lookin' for foreigners to capture and smuggle back to use as hostages."

"Sounds like a pretty tough bunch down there."

Leaning back, the big Turk copilot shouted, "Add to that, weather that changes from hot desert sandstorm," snapping his gloved fingers, "to freezing blizzard just that fast, and you got what we Turks call *Cehennem Dere!*"

"What's that mean?" shouted the back-seat rock hunter, his knuckles turning white under his gloved hands gripping the seat. The big Turk slowly swiveled his shoulders, his massive head squaring face to face with the American. With a gravelly voice, he growled, "The Gorge of Hell!"

Falling back against his seat, Bob yelled to Chuck, "And we're supposed to hunt out the Ark from that boiling pot of intrigue, danger, and death?"

"Now you got the idea," shouted Chuck over his shoulder, his eyes flashing with excitement as his red handlebar mustache framed an ear-to-ear grin. "But look at it this way, Partner, you could either be up here with us on the caldera at fifteen thousand feet, or you could be down there with Dr. Morris and the other expedition looking for clues as they work their way up the gorge. Might be blizzards and avalanches up here, but at least we know we won't be facing the terrorists and bandits hangin' out down there!"

"Great choice," mumbled the geophysicist slumping in the back seat.

The helicopter labored as it climbed through fifteen thousand feet on the west side of the snow-covered mountain that showed blush orange in the early dawn. Swinging left, they headed toward the caldera on the south face. As they approached, Chuck dropped the chopper for his first pass over the ice-filled crater's flat surface, skimming at a hundred knots ten feet off the snow.

Leaning out into the thin air, he checked the surface, making sure it was hard-packed, okay for a landing. His eyes smarted in the blasting cold air. Banking hard left, his blades a scant three feet off the snow pack, he swung out over the edge of the caldera. The mountain suddenly dropped nine thousand feet straight down from the hard-banking, doorless helicopter. Chuck glanced up and to his right at Yavuz, who raised his bushy eyebrows and broke into a huge, toothy smile behind his black mustache. Bob put his hand over his mouth, choking back his stomach as he hunkered down among the equipment piled ceiling-high. Chuck laughed, then signaled with his hand that he was going to circle and land, going forward like an airplane. Yavuz's smile disappeared behind his mustache. He grabbed for the earphones and mike. Shaking his head, he bellowed, "No land. Helicopter cannot hover above eight thousand feet. Landing impossible!"

"Sure we can, Yavuz," yelled Chuck with a grin. "Haven't you ever planted one of these babies on the run? Tell you what," he yelled, "if we shoot off the edge, I'll let you take over!" Chuck's eyes laughed as he glanced at the Turkish copilot who stared in stunned disbelief at this crazy American who was actually going to land a helicopter seven thousand feet above its capacity by flying it in and skidding to a stop. Chuck continued the hard-left bank while dropping low for the approach; an audible groan came from the back seat. Yavuz gripped the crash bar with both hands, his eyes fixed on the fast-approaching ledge four hundred meters away. The chopper's black, flashing shadow closed with the white snow pack. Geysers of snow shot from the six-inch upturned toes on the leading edges of the landing skids as the helicopter shot across the caldera, slowed, tilted precariously up, then rocked back flat.

"Nothin' to it," said Chuck, pounding Yavuz on the back, shaking him from his frozen, jaw-hanging trance. Idling the engine, Chuck cracked his seatbelt. Bob was already out, praising the Lord and unloading radar gear, tents, and crates of food. Within minutes, the three men emptied the craft. Hunched over,

Bob started to drag off gear from under the spinning blades and stake out their seven-day campsite. Chuck motioned his Turkish copilot to hop back in so they could head back down and pick up the third member of the team and the next load of gear. Before Chuck gunned the idling engine, Yavuz leaned over and said, "How you gonna take off? We much too high to go straight up!"

"Strap in and watch this," said Chuck. Applying power, the big, thirty-foot blades blurred in the severe, clear-blue sky as the jet engine screamed to an ear-shattering crescendo. Chuck first rocked the craft to break the frozen skids. Then, tilting the helicopter slightly forward on the skid toes, he gave full power, aiming dead ahead for the drop-off. Once more the big Turk's mouth dropped open; his hands gripped the crash bar; he watched with terror-filled eyes as the helicopter shot out over the caldera ledge. As the nose dropped, craft and crew rocketed straight down, a bare two hundred feet out from the sheer cliff wall.

"Yee-haa!" yelled Chuck as the helicopter gained airspeed in its free fall, the front windscreen filling with the chasm bottom nine thousand feet straight down. At a hundred knots, he got his pedals working and pulled the stick back, lifting the nose. Instantly the helicopter bottomed out and shot straight-away from the mountain. Their stomachs sank deep as the g-force sucked them into their seats. "Like I said, nothin' to it," yelled Chuck to his headshaking Turkish copilot.

Landing at base, Chuck went in to meet with the local military commander while B. J., the third team member, and Yavuz loaded for the second shuttle to the caldera. The *gendarme* commandant leaned his machine gun in the corner, then turned, and looked sternly at Chuck, motioning him to be seated across from him at his big desk. "Remember, you must check in with the *gendarme*—that's our military—at least three times a day via radio. If we don't hear from you, we have orders to send up commandos immediately. There are reports of heavy terrorist activity on both the Iraqi and Iranian borders. Americans are their number one targets, and it would disturb our president greatly if you were to be taken hostage."

As the nose dropped, craft and crew rocketed straight down.

"Really wouldn't sit too well with me either—but certainly, Commandant, you don't expect those crazies on the mountaintop!"

"Over here you'll learn one thing, if nothing else—always expect the unexpected. Many strange and mysterious things have happened on that mountain, especially to those who are searching for the greatest artifact in the world. Don't forget, only a few thousand years ago all mankind was killed except for eight on that Ark. The men who find it could become rich and famous. They would make prize hostages."

"We seek to find the Ark *only* for the glory of God," said Chuck.

"I believe you, but that puts you in deeper danger, for in addition to the greed of men, Satan will do his best to stop you. May Allah be with you." Standing, Chuck thanked the Commandant and left to meet his crew.

Four more times they shuttled their gear to the caldera. Four times they took off, dropping down the sheer mountainside to gain airspeed before stabilizing in flight. Before the last takeoff, Chuck, along with Bob and B. J., gathered around Yavuz, who sat alone in the cockpit. "Remember, Yavuz, we'll meet you back up here in seven days for our pickup. Now, fly this baby down just as we did four times before. Crank it up to full speed and go for the ledge. Hang on the drop till you've got a hundred knots; then pull the stick back, and you've got it made." With a slap on his back and a sharp "thumbs up," Chuck added while backing away, "You can do it, Yavuz, I know it."

Pointing at Chuck from the pilot's seat, Yavuz waved him back over once more and said with a grin, "You come with me, yes?"

"No," hollered Chuck over the gunning engine, shaking his head, "you gotta get yourself off the mountain."

The Turk's pleading smile faded as he turned his ashen-faced attention to the instruments and fired the engine to a roaring crescendo. Once more he looked at the three Americans, then gave them a half-hearted "thumbs up."

"Think he'll make it?"

"We'll know in about ten seconds," said Chuck as they watched the helicopter disappear over the drop-off in a cloud of snow. Silence. Then, after an eternal ten seconds, a collective cheer went up as they heard the "Whomp! Whomp! Whomp!" of blades biting air in the pullout.

Turning to their tasks, the men pitched tents, got the generator running, stashed the food, and began to lay out grid points in the snow to shoot their radar down into the thousand-foot depths of the ice. They planned to make several hundred radar shots over the next week in the hope of plotting a pattern outline of the Ark, which, according to Genesis 8:4, came to rest somewhere on the mountains of Ararat, and just might be locked deep within the caldera's ice. If they should discern a rectangular form 450 feet long and 75 feet wide, they'd then drill for core samples to confirm the find.

As the men began to pace off a grid layout, something caught the corner of Chuck's eye. Glancing up at the summit only a mile to his right, he spotted two black dots against the white snow coming down the slope toward them. Keeping his eyes on the black dots, he dropped his grid flags, bit off his right glove, half unzipped his jacket, and pulled binoculars to his eyes. Twisting the focus knob, the dots turned into men dressed in black from head to foot. The earflaps on their wool hats tossed wildly as they charged down toward them through ankle-deep snow, kicking geysers up with each pounding lurch. In one hand they carried ice axes; in the other, machine guns.

"We've got company," shouted Chuck to his teammates, who froze in disbelief, then twisting their heads, followed his gaze to the fast-approaching duo.

"Will you look at those guys poundin' through the snow!" said an astounded B. J. "I take ten paces in this thin air and I'm gaspin', and—"

"And they got machine guns, guys! This doesn't look good," said Chuck as he lowered his binoculars and nervously bit at the edge of his mustache.

The two chargers burst upon the Americans. Dropping their ice axes, they half-crouched, gripping their machine guns with both hands. The big one cautiously moved to Chuck, his eyes flashing from man to man. Hot, steamy breath shot from his flaring nostrils. Then standing up straight, chest to chest, he shoved the cold muzzle of his machine gun under

Chuck's chin, finger on the trigger. All three Americans instantly raised their hands. A stream of guttural Turkish blasted in Chuck's face. Red, bloodshot eyes flashed anger as Chuck shook his head "no," dragging the ice-cold gun barrel with his chin, trying to indicate he didn't understand Turkish. Taking a step back while keeping his quarry covered, he motioned the grubby-bearded one to the tent. Backing over, the second man hesitantly lowered his machine gun, then quickly turned and ripped open the tent and kicked out the contents. With his gun butt he smashed open equipment and food boxes. Within minutes, gear lay scattered over the expedition site. Finding the stash of candy bars, "Grubby Beard" stuffed his pockets, then bit into one, chewing paper and all.

The big one screamed at Chuck again, his red eyes flashing as saliva dribbled down the five-day stubble of black whiskers, his black mustache barely inches from Chuck's red handlebar mustache. The candy-bar chomper moved over and ripped the video camera from Bob's shoulder strap. He expertly opened the camera, took out the tape, and smashed it on

"We've got company."

the snow, grinding it in with his heel. Chuck glanced down past his nose at the machine gun muzzle forcing his chin up. On it was stamped "G-3"—the same make as the Commandant's. Then, just for a second, he caught a glimpse of an insignia on a shirt under the black jacket of "Red Eyes." Could it be? With his hands still held high, he gingerly pointed one finger toward the man's collar and with a hoarse voice asked, *"Gendarme*?" The big Turk stopped yelling, looked at Chuck sideways and took a suspicious step back, still pointing his weapon squarely between Chuck's eyes. Dropping one hand slightly, Chuck pointed to the half-hidden, military insignia, *"Gendarme*?" Slowly, the Turk nodded up and down. An audible hiss of relief went out from all three Americans.

Nodding his head to the radio transmitter lying on the snow, Chuck said, "Commandant *gendarme*—radio." Stepping back, the big Turk motioned with his gun barrel toward the radio. Slowly, Chuck bent down and picked up the radio with one hand while keeping the other up high. Keeping his eyes fixed on his nervous captor, he pushed the mike button and called,

"*Gendarme* Commandant, *gendarme*, this is Aaron on the caldera. Commandant, if you can read me, come in. Over." Click! Silence. "Red Eyes" moved a step forward, raising his gun to his shoulder. His partner bit off another hunk of paper-wrapped Snickers and slowly munched, his steel eyes fixed on Chuck.

Louder this time, "*Commandant, come in.*"

B. J. whispered from behind Chuck, "Be there, man, be there . . . this is it. Please, Lord, let him be there."

A crackle, then static, then loud and clear, "Go ahead, Aaron, this is the Commandant at base. Over."

"We've got two guys up here with machine guns pointed at us. I think they're military. That is, I hope they're military—man, I'm prayin' they're military! You'd better talk to them and tell them we're friendlies. Things are gettin' mighty hairy up here!"

"I understand your situation. Put one of them on."

Slowly, Chuck handed the radio transmitter to the big one. Taking a step forward, he shoved the G-3 in Chuck's belly with his right hand; with his left he took the transmitter.

"*Allo*?" A stream of Turkish flashed from the radio. The red-eyed Turk turned his attention to the transmitter; the machine gun dropped slowly from Chuck's belly.

Chuck eased his arms down, putting his hands into his big outer jacket pockets as if to keep them warm. His mind flashed, *Just in case these guys aren't military. . . .* The fingers of his right hand gripped the loaded twelve-gauge flare gun concealed inside. He had only one shot, but if he could line up both men, he was sure the burning phosphorus shell would go right through both of them at this close range. He pointed the pocket-concealed barrel at the radio talker's belly and took a slow step sideways, lining up both men. Then, as his thumb started to ease back the hammer, the red-eyed radioman yelled something to his partner and turned to Chuck with a huge grin. Slinging his machine gun across his back on its strap, he cocked his head, held out his arms with palms up, and loudly said, "*Amerikali, evet*?"

Chuck said, "American, yes."

Stepping over, "Red Eyes" threw his arms around Chuck in a huge bear hug, giving him a rough whisker kiss on both cheeks. Then

"Commandant, come in."

stepping back, he whacked Chuck on both shoulders with his hands, turned, and proceeded to give the other two Americans his big bear hug and bristled-cheek kiss. The candy-bar muncher followed suit. When the whacks and kisses were over, the two Turks picked up their ice axes, laughed loudly, gave a grand wave, turned, and proceeded to run back up the snow pack toward the summit. The three Americans watched in stunned silence from the gear-strewn campsite as the black dots disappeared over the snow cornices toward the summit.

B. J. broke the awed stillness, "Can you believe that? I mean, these guys come outta nowhere ready to kill us. Then they turn into our greatest buddies. Then they disappear like the Lone Ranger and Tonto in a cloud of dust, running—actually running—uphill. I can't believe them. They just aren't human!"

"Thank the Lord they weren't terrorists, either," said Chuck, easing his thumb back on the hammer of the twelve-gauge in his pocket.

CHAPTER 2

S weat ran down the chests of the men on the north face assault team, soaking their shirts to the waist. Trudging single file with heads down, the three men forced their way up the crumbling rock foothills of the Ahora Gorge in the searing, hot afternoon sun, the straps on their eighty-pound backpacks cutting into flesh beneath shirts worn thin from days of packing on the rock-hard trail.

Over the past year, the hand-picked team, led by geologist-explorer Dr. John Morris, had individually honed their muscles blue-steel hard by jogging, weight lifting, and countless iron man sit-ups. Together they climbed the Sierra Madres of California and the icy walls of Mount Rainier in Washington. Around the evening campfires, "Big John," as his expedition mates called him, had poured out his ten years of research on Mount Ararat and the Ark that lay hidden somewhere on its heights. Mentally and physically prepared, the men were resolutely determined that not one of the huge obstacles they faced would stop them—not the searing heat, the bitter cold, the avalanches, not even the terrorists. But now, a bare two days out . . .

"Pinworms," coughed John, "I've got 'Ataturk's Revenge'!" He spat the words out in disgust as the trail spun in front of his bleary eyes, his body wracked with nausea and cramps. Staggering, he signaled a halt to the two men following. Dropping his head, he leaned heavily on his walking staff with both hands as sweat ran off his nose, splattering on the rocks. Then, as he hung gripping his staff, the still air suddenly filled with unseen tension. Cocking an ear, John heard—better yet, felt—the low, guttural rumble. Holding their breath with pounding hearts, all three men slowly turned their heads toward the primeval sound coming from the rock ledge ten paces to the left. The rumble turned into a gut-wrenching snarl as first one, then another huge head framed by massive shoulders emerged from between the boulders. Ears laid back, hair straight on end, the dreaded wolf dogs of Ararat had declared their turf. The first beast fixed his eyes on Don's jugular; foam dripped down two-inch fangs bared by snarling lips. All three men instinctively raised their ice axes and poised for the charge. For one terrifying minute the mad dogs gnashed, lurched, and snarled; then, as John and the other men began to beat their ice axes on boulders, the massive heads and jaws, still snarling and snapping, slowly slunk back down, the beasts disappearing into the maze of crevasses and rocks covering the area. Tentatively, the men lowered their ice axes.

Hissing out air, John knelt to one knee, then dropped to his rear, pushing back his sweat-soaked leather hat. Draping his sun-blackened arms over his knees, he stared down at the murky, pinworm-carrying stream that ran down the donkey trail toward the village somewhere in the valley far below.

"I think I got the pinworms day before yesterday when I accepted that drink of warm goat's milk from the villager down there," he said, nodding down the slope. "I didn't want to offend him by refusing it—I'll betcha the cup was used for drinking water first—and now I'm payin' for it." Choking, he dropped his head between his knees, his stomach convulsing.

Walking over, Brian dropped to one knee, wiping his forehead with a sweat-soaked arm while scanning the area. "It's a cinch we can't go on with you like this. Two days of diarrhea and the dry heaves would knock out the best of men. We'd better make camp and hole up for a while—see if you can't heal. For starters, we could sure use something cold."

"Here, take this," came a clear voice ringing out from behind a boulder. The startled men looked up as a young lad stepped out and walked toward them with outstretched hands cupping a huge, white mound.

"The kid's got snow—delicious, pure snow!" said Brian as he stood with a surprised laugh.

The smiling, dark-haired boy, dressed in a tattered shirt and baggy wool pants, walked from man to man, offering each a portion of his precious prize. Taking a fistful, John held it above his upturned head and squeezed, letting the ice-cold drops fall on his raw, sunburned nose, run down over his cracked lips, and trickle into his parched mouth, savoring each delicious drop. Rubbing the rest of the snow on the back of his burning neck, "Big John" squinted sideways at the lad, "We accept your gift with many thanks. What's your name and where did you come from?"

"My name is Ali, and," pointing a skinny arm, the barefoot lad continued, "while tending sheep up there on the ridge, I watched you come from far down the valley. I ran back to my grandfather's tent and told him three men approached, coming up the trail. At first, he thought you might be bandits; but when I told him you carried no guns, he sent me to fetch snow from the earthen dugout and run to welcome you. He invites you to his tent that lies over the ridge to have food with him." Pulling up his baggy pants, the barefoot lad stood proud and said, "Grandfather is *Muhtar*; he is Chief."

Leaning heavily with one hand on his staff while pushing the ground with his other, John groaned as he rose to his full height. Then, clutching his stomach with a fist, he gritted his teeth and said, "Go tell your grandfather we are Americans and seek to find the lost Ark of Noah. Tell him we come in peace and would be honored to break bread with the *Muhtar*."

Stepping back, the wide-eyed young lad stared up at the huge American towering over him. "I go quickly to tell my grandfather you come. He will fix you medicine that will take away the mountain sickness that shakes your body." Turning, he started to run, then momentarily stopped and shouted over his shoulder, "The *Muhtar* knows many secrets that are hidden in the black gorge. He knows much of the Ark you search for." Once again turning, he darted off, leaving the men's appetite whetted for food and stories of the Ark.

As the sun slipped behind the mighty snow-covered mountain, it set off an alpenglow, coloring the landscape surrounding the striped nomad's tent with a golden light. With folded arms, the old *Muhtar* stood ramrod straight in front of his tent. He was dressed in black from the turban on his head to the slippers on his feet, save for the large, curved knife in its solid gold sheath on his belt. As the

*The old Muhtar stood ramrod
straight in front of his tent.*

men approached, he fixed each with a piercing gaze from deep-set eyes. His frown turned to cautious acceptance when he saw the small American flags sewn on the backpacks that dropped to the ground from weary shoulders. After watching the men bow from the waist in respect, the old chief offered his huge, callused hand, giving each man a firm, single, up-and-down handshake. "You hunger. Ali has chosen his prized lamb for you. A feast awaits within. Welcome! Now you will enter my tent."

Turning, the men followed the *Muhtar's* lead by first taking off their boots, then bowing from the waist before entering the dark interior of the nomad's tent. The *Muhtar* walked around the flaming fire pit with the roasting lamb turning on a spit tended by his wife. Following his lead, they crossed their legs and sat down on the thick, diamond-patterned *jaffi* rug. The woman stood, her gaily patterned dress with brass beads and many gold bracelets tinkling as she poured hot *cay* from a large brass teapot and offered it to John. He politely refused. Again she offered; again he refused. On the third offer, he graciously accepted the cup. Turning and looking at the smiling *Muhtar*, John said, "We are honored to break bread with so great and wise a chief."

"You have learned the customs of the Kurds well," said the aged chief, returning the cup-of-tea salute. As he carved off slabs of hot lamb, his wife filled their plates with freshly baked bread and cups of yogurt. Ali entered with a skewer of lamb liver. Kneeling in respect, he waited for the *Muhtar's* nod, then twisted it slowly over the blue-hot part of the flame till the dripping fat and meat caught fire. Quickly, he blew out the flames, stood, reached over and pushed the pieces off on John's plate with his knife.

"Eat all of that," said the chief as he licked his fingers dripping with fat. "It will cure your mountain sickness." Brian's and Don's eyes tracked to John's plate and the chunks of liver as he gingerly picked up one of the burnt-on-the-outside, raw-in-the-middle pieces with his fingers. Hesitantly, he put the chunk in his mouth and chewed. Surprisingly, it tasted sweet. He nodded a "not bad" look at a wide-eyed Don and Brian, smiled at Ali, and quickly devoured the meat on his plate, washing it down with a great goblet of pure, ice-cold goat's milk.

The *Muhtar* nodded approval as the men ate, each being careful to suck the marrow from the bones as is the Kurdish custom. "At first light you will be strong for your search. And now," *Muhtar* declared as his black, heavy eyebrows lowered, "I will tell you stories passed down through generations from the ancient ones about *Gemi*, or the Ark, as you call it. It is the duty of *Muhtar* to carry on these stories." Ali sat cross-legged, his eyes staring across the dancing flames in wide admiration for his grandfather. The old man nodded toward his grandson, "In seasons to come, Ali will be *Muhtar*, and he must pass on the stories of the ancient ones."

Sitting ramrod-straight, the *Muhtar* spread his arms out; the black shirt sleeves dropped down from his arms like the wings of a giant black falcon, his weathered hands outstretched over the fire. He spoke with a heavy, hushed voice, "Because man was evil, God caused water to cover the earth. On it floated *Gemi* with Noah, his wife, and their sons with their wives—eight people and two, or seven, of all the animals in the world. During the Flood, God made this mighty Mount Ararat to rise through the water, and this is where they landed. When Noah left the Gemi, he made an altar and sacrificed with fire the best animals to God in thanks for delivering them from the death all mankind had suffered. Noah and his family lived in caves high on the mountain. Then, after many seasons," the old man paused and slowly pulled out his golden knife, raised it high with both hands, and made a sweeping, downward slash, pointing at the fire, then said with a powerful voice, "the mountain was split by the dagger of Satan reaching for the cave people. But God protected His people and moved them safely through the searing heat left by Satan's dagger to the foothills below. What was left was the *Cehennem Dere*—the Gorge of Hell. Some people went south to become the dwellers of the deserts, some went north to the forests, some went east to the sea, and some stayed on the mountain slopes." The *Muhtar* paused, then fixed his eyes on the dancing flames, "It is we, the Kurds, the ancient descendants of Noah's son Shem, that live in these foothills. We are the keepers of the mountain and its secrets."

Looking up, he pointed a gnarled finger at John, "I believe you when you say you seek the Ark only for the glory of God, or Allah, as we call the Almighty One. It is for this reason that I tell you the mystery of the hidden Ark." Sliding the golden dagger back into its sheath, he placed his hands on his knees and breathed deeply, collecting wisdom from his innermost being. "For you to find the *Gemi*, you must enter the black gorge and find the cave of the two ancient ones that guard the entrance to the dead. Then, going further into the gorge, you will find the stone of eight—by that you know your path is true. High above the stone of eight, you will find the altar of sacrifice."

Sweeping his arms toward the ceiling, his eyes rolled white as he looked up into the darkness of the tent. Again, in a powerful voice, "Above that, hidden in the snow, lies *Gemi*." All three men sat in awed silence, eyes fixed on the chief who sat across the bed of red embers. Slowly lowering his eyes and outstretched arms, he whispered to the coals, "Once in many generations, when the sun is high and the winter snows have been light, the ice that holds *Gemi* melts back and reveals the front of the mighty Ark. Some of our people have seen this thing, few have returned alive to tell of it." Leaning his black-turbaned head forward, he fixed his eyes on Dr. Morris, paused, then said in a heavy, hushed voice, "And I, *Muhtar*, am one of them!"

Leaning back, he breathed deeply, then continued, "Tomorrow, before first light, Ali will lead you into the black gorge and up to the entrance of *Cehennem Dere*. There you can make base camp. Ali will stay there and keep watch over your things and wait for your return. He must go no further into the Gorge of Hell, for he is too young to face the *djinn* that live in the upper reaches of the gorge. These evil spirits work harm on all who search for *Gemi*, for they know that if the Ark is found, many will believe God and turn from their evil ways and worship the God of all creation." Leaning back into the shadows, the *Muhtar* spoke gently but firmly, "The black gorge will not give up its secrets easily. You will need all your strength and the strength of God. Allah be with you, my brothers."

CHAPTER 3

High on the ice-covered caldera, the men on the south face expedition laid grids and shot their radar, probing deep into the glacier looking for signs of the Ark. For three exhausting days they systematically worked across the caldera, eliminating a major portion, and now they closed in on the final section where the Ark could be trapped. Moving the heavy equipment in the thin air on that particular afternoon had pushed the men to their limits. Then, with a front moving in, the radio crackled to life, with the gravelly voice of the *gendarme* Commandant. Chuck hurried to the tent and picked up the radio. Puffing, he more gasped than spoke, "This is caldera. Go ahead, base."

"This is an urgent message. You must get off the mountain of Ararat immediately. We have just received word that a pack of PKK terrorists are moving up the north face of the mountain. Our informer has told us that they intend to surprise and attack your outpost. These men want no hostages—they are killers; your lives are in jeopardy, you must leave immediately. Do you understand? Over."

Gripping the transmitter, Chuck looked up and waved at Bob and B. J. working the equipment two hundred meters out. "Roger, base, read you loud and clear. We are to prepare to leave immediately. We'll get our essential gear ready. By the time Yavuz gets here in the helicopter, we'll be prepared to leave. Over."

"Ah, roger, caldera, I thought you would say that. One moment while I open this. I have a message for you from the helicopter pilot—let me read it to you. 'To Expedition Leader Aaron: I'll meet you at the eight-thousand-foot level. Get yourself off the mountain. Signed, Yavuz.' This means he doesn't want to fly the helicopter above the limits of its capability, and I cannot force him to do so. You'll have to climb down to eight thousand feet. Remember, come down the south face—the bandits are coming up the north face. May Allah be with you." Click!

Lowering the radio, Chuck shook his head in disbelief as the other men huffed up. "You're not gonna believe this. That was the Commandant—he said we've got to leave immediately. Terrorists are coming up the north face, and they're comin' after us!"

"We better get crackin' and have Yavuz fly up here fast," said Bob, scanning the sky that was beginning to drop huge snowflakes.

"You haven't heard the best part. Yavuz is chicken to fly up and land!"

"What?" said both men at once, looking in shock at Chuck.

"Yeah, he left us a note—said, 'Get yourself off the mountain. Signed, Yavuz.'"

"Has a familiar ring to it, doesn't it?" said B. J. stomping his cold feet while nervously scanning the summit.

"Let's take stock, guys. It's late in the day—at best, we have two, maybe three, hours of light. We've got no weapons but a flare gun. The bandits are coming up the north face; it's nine thousand feet straight down the south face. And there's bad weather moving in."

"I suggest we do some heavy, fast prayin'," said Bob. Nodding agreement, all three men bowed their heads. "Lord, we are three guys in deep trouble. Please help guide us to safety."

Looking up, B. J. said, "Let's get our ice axes and what weapons we can make do and show these guys we mean to make a stand. Then let's pool what money we've got, and as a last resort, maybe we can buy 'em off."

"Fat chance. They'll blow us away and take our bucks anyway!" spit Bob.

"Look, man, you got a better idea, then I'm listenin'," said a tight-lipped B. J.

"Lighten up, guys. Let's use our heads. First off, load a light pack each in case we can make a break around the enemy in the dark and head down the north face," said Chuck, looking more for time to think than expediency.

As the men scrambled to pack essentials, B. J. looked up, "Hang on, it may be too late—look at that!" All three men straightened and stared through the fading snow as a lone, gray figure approached in the distance. Chuck fumbled for his binoculars.

"Is it a friendly or a bandit?" said Bob, squinting into the snow.

"I'm not sure, but the guy appears to be alone and he isn't carryin' a machine gun."

The three men stood and watched the stranger silently come toward them through the softly falling snow. As he drew closer he stopped, then raised a bare hand, the international sign for peace. After a pause, he silently moved forward. Up close now, he stopped. They could see a soft smile; no one moved as they stared at the slender man. He wore a black stocking cap pulled over his ears; hanging loosely from his tall frame was a patched, gray tweed, Western-style, two-piece suit. Underneath was a collarless wool undershirt buttoned once at the neck. On his feet were dirty-white, ankle-high tennis shoes. He wore no socks, no gloves, no coat. Behind high cheekbones and a two-day stubble of whiskers were dark, deep-set, sympathetic eyes.

Silently walking past the men, he motioned them with a callused hand to follow as he paced toward the caldera ledge a hundred meters out. Reaching the drop-off, he squatted on his haunches. The three cautious men, with backpacks and ice axes, came up and stood behind him. Looking down into the abyss, the stranger's eyes swung to his left following the sixty-degree ice wall that led five hundred feet over to a finger-point of black volcanic rock. The rock formed a wedge that descended toward the valley somewhere below in the swirling snow. Twisting his head, he held out a hand and motioned for Chuck's ice ax. Chuck hesitantly handed it to him handle first.

Taking the ax, the stranger reached down and chipped out a notch. Then, twisting his face to the wall, he swung his lanky leg out over the ledge, slipped his tennis shoe into the notch, and put his left hand on the inward-slanting ice wall. At waist-high, he cut a second notch, smaller than the first. Then gripping his hand in that notch, he bent down, reached out, and chipped out a second foothold two feet over. Standing up while leaning into the ice wall and balancing himself on his left foot, he moved his right to the second foot slot, bent down, and cut another notch an ax-handle width over. Again standing, he looked back, smiled slightly, and nodded for the men to follow.

He stopped, then raised a bare hand,
the international sign for peace.

"Wait a minute, this guy actually wants us to follow him in a traverse across the ice wall to the rocks. I mean, some guy appears out of nowhere in a tweed suit, tennis shoes, no socks, says nothin', and then, with his bare hands and an ice ax, proceeds to chip out holds and shinny across a sheer, nine-thousand-foot drop-off—we've no ice crampons, no rope, no clamps. And further, we don't even know if he's a terrorist or what. Man, this is absolutely wild!" exclaimed B. J.

"You bet your life it's wild," said Chuck over the rising wind, "but the way I figure it, we're running outta everything—time, weather, and light. We really don't have much of a choice—it's either sit here and face the terrorists, or follow 'Tennis Shoes' across the ice wall. Something in my gut says we've gotta trust this guy; and as expedition leader, I say we follow him." Chuck twisted to face the wall, then swung a leg out over the ledge, feeling with his foot for the first notch.

Once more bending down, the stranger reached out and chipped the next series of toe notches. One by one the men followed, placing their toes into the chipped slots, leaning slightly forward into the slanting ice wall, bracing themselves with hands against the ice. In minutes all four men were sidestepping in a left to right, step-by-step traverse across the ice face. For forty-five minutes they hugged the wall, clinging to life in five-inch toeholds. With his cheek to the ice, Chuck watched the stranger time after time methodically bend down, get a hold with his bare left hand, and then with his right hand gripping the ice ax, reach out and chip out the next foothold. Step-by-step, the four tiny, dark figures edged their way across the mammoth caldera ice face in the fast-darkening sky.

Stretching for his next toehold, Bob's foot slipped. He jerked hard, switching his weight back to his left foot. The ice ax slipped from his backpack, bounced once against the ice wall, twisted wildly, and disappeared into the snow-swirling black abyss.

"Don't look down," yelled Chuck as Bob hugged the wall, clinging precariously while his foot thrashed, searching for the toehold. Finding it, he equalized his weight. Then, pumping out jets of steamy breath, he looked at Chuck, his cheek hugging the ice. Neither man spoke as their eyes locked on each other, their hearts beating hard against the ice. After a moment's respite, Chuck turned his face back to the ice-chipping stranger barely visible a scant ten feet over. Gathering their courage while fighting off fatigue and bitter cold, the men once again set off on the side-step traverse. Then, just as darkness closed and the wind turned to a howl, Chuck saw the outstretched arm of the stranger reaching for him from snow-covered rocks. With a death grip, he clasped the hand and took his last step to safely.

One by one, the exhausted climbers reached the rocky haven. Collapsing against the boulders, the men sat elbows on knees. With heads down and chests heaving, they sucked great gulps of the rare air. After a moment, the tall stranger, still standing, motioned them to follow. Rising slowly, the men followed his lead down through the maze of rocks and crevasses. For an hour they stumbled on; then, too exhausted to continue, Chuck held up his hand and flopped back in the recesses of black volcanic rock.

*For forty-five minutes they hugged the wall,
clinging to life in five-inch toeholds.*

Looking up at the now-dark stranger, Chuck said, "Mister, I don't know who you are, but we can't go a step further. We're gonna break out the sleeping bags right here and bed down." Reaching over, he broke the strap on his backpack, "Here, take one; we've got an extra." With his heart pounding hard, he continued, "We've gotta be safe now. There's no way those terrorists can traverse that ice wall in the dark. Frankly, I don't know how we did it." Looking up, he squinted one eye while shaking his head and said louder, "Did you understand anything I said? *Amliyormusan? Verstehen sie? Comprende?*"

The stranger turned from looking down the mountain, his dark eyes fixed on Chuck. Silently, he bent over, placing the ice ax against a boulder. Then standing straight, he lifted a bare hand, took a step back into the swirling snow, and disappeared into the darkness.

B. J. echoed the thoughts of the other two exhausted men as they crawled into their down sleeping bags, "If that isn't the strangest thing a man has ever seen." Shaking his head as he pulled the cocoon top up, he gave out a muffled, "That was just a miracle—no other way to explain it!"

Chuck closed his eyes and thanked the Lord for guiding them to safety. Just before sleep enveloped him, he thought with envy of John and the other expedition team on the warm, lower slopes of the north side of the mountain looking for clues to the Ark's location. *Those lucky dudes!*

ଊ ଊ ଊ

Bob awoke with a jerk. A bare hand gripped his mouth. Chuck released him, then raised a finger to his lips for quiet, pointing to the blackness at their right. Scrunching up, Bob squinted into the night. Through the blowing snow, he saw a flicker of light, then another. Hearing a rock crunch behind, the duo spun around; more flashlights flickered to their left.

"Terrorists?" whispered Bob. Chuck raised his palm in a "maybe" sign.

Hunkering down deep in the rocks, the men watched the flickering lights proceed up the mountain on either side of them, not fifty feet away. For a minute they held their breath;

then the lights disappeared up the slope into the howling wind.

The men slept fitfully the rest of the night. Then as the dawn started to break—"*Allo-o-o! Allo-o-o!*" The three men twisted to their knees and peered over the top of the boulder, looking downhill. Collective smiles broke out on their weathered faces as they spotted the lanky stranger smiling back up at them from under his black stocking cap. Once again the three men set out, following the man in the patched tweed suit and white tennis shoes. Down he led them for the better part of ten hours, down through the mass of crevasses and crumbly rock ledges. He walked with the surefooted strides of a man who knew his way, yet there were no trails, no markers, only a mass of boulders and crumbled, snow-covered rock.

Toward late afternoon, the now-dehydrated, exhausted men rounded a huge volcanic boulder and came face to face with the helicopter. Yavuz smiled broadly at them from the cockpit. Walking over, Chuck leaned in and looked at the altimeter. "Let me guess. Yup, eight thousand feet!" Shaking his head, he looked sideways at the big Turk. "Well, Yavuz, I guess I gotta tell you I'm mighty happy to see your big ugly face, no matter what!" The two men broke out laughing, then hugged and slapped each other on the back.

Throwing their packs in, the other men clambered on board as Yavuz hit the starter switch and fired up the engine. The big blades began to whip; after he buckled his seatbelt, Chuck looked out the front windshield. There stood the tall stranger fifty paces over. Leaning out, he shouted at him through the side door while waving for him to join them. The tall, slender man just raised his hand in farewell and smiled. As Yavuz took off, the swirling snow obscured the ground. Hovering at a hundred feet, Chuck motioned for the Turkish pilot to swing around.

Nodding, Yavuz swung the chopper to face the mountain. All four men looked down. The stranger was gone. A hand gripped Chuck's shoulder. "Must have walked off through the rocks back there or somethin'," shouted B. J., leaning forward from his seat.

"Yeah," said Chuck, adding under his breath, "or somethin'." Yavuz shrugged, then swung hard left and banked down the mountain toward base.

ಽಂ   ಽಂ   ಽಂ

Tilting back on the hind legs of his chair, the Commandant of the *gendarme* studied the ten-inch knife he twisted between his hands. After listening intently for thirty minutes to their account, he looked past the knife and spoke slowly and deliberately to the expedition team seated in front of his huge cedar desk. "The flashlights you saw coming up the mountain last night were my commandos. They must have passed you about midnight, because an hour later they scaled the ice wall. Once on top, they snuck up on your camp, surprising four terrorists." Leaning forward, he jabbed the knife into the desktop with a thud and growled, "A firefight broke out, and my men killed all four of them. Later, they continued on to the summit and are now sweeping the north face for any additional bandits." Yanking the knife out, he leaned back and said with a shrug, "As for your special guide in the tweed suit, I have no idea who he was. I assure you, he was not one of my men. My guess is, he was a well-meaning Kurd." Pointing his knife at Chuck, he raised his eyebrows, "Remember, Mr. Aaron, what I told you about the savage mountain. Mysterious things happen up there. But the one thing you can count on for sure—expect the unexpected."

Standing, Chuck reached out to shake the Commandant's hand, "We'll be taking off in the helicopter now to rendezvous with Dr. Morris and his team on the north foothills." Turning to go, Chuck stopped, turned slightly and said over his shoulder, "You know, Commandant, you're absolutely right about the savage mountain, especially about expecting the unexpected. With a bit more faith, maybe the faith of a mustard seed, we should have expected our tall stranger—after all, we asked for him!"

CHAPTER 4

Ali stood atop the rock ledge above the tents and gear of base camp and gave one more wave to the men of the north expedition team as they disappeared far up the trail leading to the upper reaches of the black gorge. Once more, under the searing sun, the three men labored single file through the stifling canyon heat. By high noon, their hiking boots squished with sweat at each trudging step.

Halting for a break, John and Don leaned back against a boulder while Brian scampered on top, searching the canyon walls with binoculars. John reached in his pocket for some beef jerky. "Yeow! That hurt!" He held up a puffed, sun-blistered hand.

"I've got the same problem," said Don, pouring his canteen over the back of his lowered head, letting the water run down his whiskered face. Shaking his head in a spray, he held out the black, snow-filled canteen, "Here, pour some of this on your hands. It's still cool."

As John sloshed the canteen over his hands, Brian called out, "I think I might have spotted something up here." Pointing with one hand up the canyon wall while shading his eyes with the other, he called over his shoulder, "Look up there, guys; see that tiny black dot? That just might be the entrance to a cave. If you look closely, you can make out a kinda thread leading from it along the canyon wall back down to the floor over there. My guess is that's a path or stair ledge leading up to a cave. What do ya' think, John, is this the cave the old *Muhtar* talked about?"

Shading his eyes with cupped hands, John squinted into the sun. "Just might be, at least it's worth a try. You lead the way, Brian."

Three-quarters of the way up the canyon wall, the team rounded a ledge. Brian held up a hand for them to stop. Dropping his arm, he pointed ten paces forward to where the man-made rock

*The three men labored single file
through the stifling canyon heat.*

staircase narrowed, then came to an abrupt end. A hundred feet over, it continued on up and over to the now-visible cave entrance.

"Something smashed the walkway, probably a rock slide comin' from up there on the lip," nodded Brian while slipping off his backpack and handing it back to John. Getting down on hands and knees, he edged to the break. Leaning over, he studied the cliff wall and a crack that ran the length of the knocked-out stairway, then said, "I can make it across."

"Are you sure, Brian? It's seven hundred feet straight down, and the crack you've got to work with doesn't look like the best fingerhold to me," said Don as John shook his head.

"No sweat. I tackled a lot tougher ones than this on Mount Rainier. Gimme a crack and I can go anywhere!" he grinned, spitting on his hands and rubbing them in anticipation. Facing the wall, he reached out and inserted his right-hand fingers into the crack that ran the length of the gap. Leaning out, he edged his left-hand fingers along the crack; then gripping with both hands, he swung his legs out, his feet scratching for tiny toeholds. For twenty minutes the men called encouragement as they watched him work his way across, literally hanging by his fingers.

"Watch it, Brian!" was all John could shout before a small gravel and dirt slide cascaded from the lip and rained off the climber's bare knuckles and leather hat.

"You okay?" shouted the two men in unison, their voices echoing down the canyon wall.

Spitting dirt, the clinging rock climber hung straight-armed for a second, his rippling shoulder muscles showing through his gritty, sweat-soaked shirt. "Wouldn't be any fun without a slide or two," he shouted back over his shoulder, stretching for his next hold.

Shaking his head, Don said, "The guy's half mountain goat!"

"Nope, you're wrong—he's all mountain goat!" said John, watching Brian step lightly on the continuing rock-ledge staircase. "Atta boy, Brian. Go get 'em now; we'll wait here."

Reaching the three-foot-square entrance to the cave, Brian pulled a flashlight from his hip pocket and cautiously poked his head into the jet-black interior. Switching on the light, he flashed the beam around a low-ceilinged chamber. Pulling back out, he yelled, "It's man-made, all right. The walls are handcarved. I'm goin' in." With a "thumbs up" from John, he pulled himself through the entrance and dropped lightly to the silt-covered floor in a crouch. Playing the light in a circle, he made out two cobwebbed doorways; he chose the one to the left and crawled over, holding the flashlight in his mouth. Reaching out, he hesitantly pulled the mass of spider webs aside and cautiously peered in. Moving his head, the light circled the small room, then slowly played across an eight-foot-long stone object lying in the center. "Here goes nothin'," he grunted. Crawling on all fours, the mouth-held light flashed across the two-foot-high stone, boxlike object. Putting his hands on the edge, he pulled up with both hands. His eyes grew wide; then grabbing the flashlight out of his mouth, he let out a low whistle, "Will you look at this! It's a sarcophagus—an honest-to-goodness stone coffin!"

Backing out of the first side room, he turned around on his hands and knees, making for the bright light shining through the cave entrance door. Then glancing to his left, he halted, looking at the other web-covered

"It's a sarcophagus—an honest-to-goodness stone coffin!"

passageway. "Yeah, why not?" Crawling over, he reached out. "These spider webs really give me the creeps!" Once again peering in, he could see a crudely cut staircase descending around a black corner. He started to go in, then hesitating, said, "Should I, or shouldn't I?" With a roar, the ancient, hewn staircase ceiling gave way, sending tons of silt smashing down the staircase. "Got my answer—I'm outta here," he shouted scrambling backwards on flailing hands and knees into the dust-choked main room. Spinning around, his eyes groped for the now-dim light of the cave entrance. Squirming, he thrust himself half out, gasping for air. Dropping to his feet at the cave ledge entrance, he stood spitting the dirt and cobwebs out of his mouth and beating the silt off his pants with his cobweb-covered leather hat.

"You okay?" bellowed John, looking at the blackened figure standing at the dust-belching cave entrance.

"Yeah, but enough is enough! Soon as my eyes adjust, I'm comin' back." Turning from the brilliant sunlight, he leaned an elbow against the side of the cave entrance and wiped his tearing eyes with a thumb and forefinger. As his eyes cleared and focused, he looked at the rock wall. "What's this?" Shaking his head, he dropped to his knees and began to brush the silt-covered wall. "How about that!" he shouted as he rose, vigorously brushing the wall with both hands. Standing full height, he tilted back the brim on his hat, put his hands on his hips, and let out a whistle while looking at the stone carving.

"What do you have, Brian?" yelled Don.

"It's a carving on the left face of the entrance." Again rubbing vigorously, he shouted, "It's a guy in a turban and long robe—and yeah, he's holding a staff." Quickly stepping to the other side, he again rubbed. "I've got the same thing over here." Then standing on his tiptoes, he swatted the stone face above the entrance with his hat. "I can make out somethin' up here. It's a four-legged animal, maybe a bull. Looks like it's cut in half and the head's missing. This is it, guys. This has gotta be the cave old *Muhtar* was talkin' about!"

ဢ   ဢ   ဢ

Sitting around the small campfire at their forward campsite that night, the three men stared into the flames. Looking across at John, Don said excitedly, "That cave certainly was man-made by early dwellers. What do you make of it, John? Think we should put any stock in the old man's story?"

"I'm not positive right now, Don. One thing's sure, though. If we find that stone of eight and the altar, I'd say we're well on our way to proving his tale; and it just might be the Ark is sittin' half-covered in snow somewhere on the mountain face. What do you think, Brian? You're the guy that got the close-up of the coffin and the carvings on the cave wall."

Leaning forward, Brian pulled his sleeping bag over his legs and drew it up to his chin. "Right now I'm so tuckered out, all I can think about are those lucky guys up on the nice cool caldera snuggled in tents, probably chowing down on a hot meal flown in special by their Turkish pilot. Man, they've got it made! Good night, folks."

"It's a guy in a turban and long robe."

"Wake up, wake up! Wake up, you guys!" yelled Don, charging into camp as the first streams of sunlight cracked the eastern foothills.

"Oh, man, I coulda slept all day," groaned Brian rolling over. "This better be good, like sourdough pancakes and bacon, or somethin'."

"Better than that," shouted Don. "I was hikin' up the ridge to get a view as the sun was breaking, and as I climbed on top of this flat rock I looked down and there it was!"

"Was what?" yawned a mildly interested John.

"What do ya' mean, 'what'? I found it, right smack in front of me—on the very stone I used to boost myself up were some carvings. I think I found the stone of eight!" The campsite exploded. Grabbing pants, Brian and John started to question their expedition mate as they scrambled to stuff sleeping bags and break camp. Within minutes the team was following Don's long strides up the ridge. Topping a stone outcrop, Don stopped, scanned the area, then huffing, said, "Up there—just a bit higher—we can actually follow this old pathway between boulders. Come on, we're gettin' close."

Rounding a black volcanic boulder, Don dropped to his knees and pulled back a stand of waist-high weeds from in front of a large, upright, flat-surfaced rock. "Big John" slowly stepped forward and squatted down. Tilting his hat back, he let his finger gently trace the eight crosses neatly carved on the stone face in a heart-shaped pattern. He whispered softly, "By the way they are worn, we certainly know they are ancient." His mind whirled, then he said out loud, "The design cut is definitely Sumerian."

Don nodded downhill and said, "I found single markers down there—spread out in a semicircle—with this one up here more or less the head of them all. Each of the smaller ones had a single cross on it. To me, it sorta looks like a—"

"Like an ancient burial ground," cut in John, stroking the sweat off his chin whiskers. In deep concentration, he fixed his eyes on the eight crosses, then nodded, "Yup, my guess is this marks the spot where the first and most prominent eight of the group were buried."

The momentary stillness was broken as Brian charged down the slope kicking stones as he skidded around the boulder. "You guys, over here—quick!" Stopping, he put his hands on his knees and gulped air. Looking up, he huffed, "There's a crude stone path over there goin' up to a mammoth flat rock, and it's got some sorta man-made structure on it. Just might be—" huffing again as John and Don stood upright, "might be the sacrificial altar!"

Scrambling up the path, the men reached a huge flat, circular area. After catching their breath, they slowly and silently paced past a crumbled stone structure to the ledge. Brian let out a low whistle as they stared over the sprawling, black, Ahora Gorge that spread, then cascaded down, into the hazy valley miles below. Slowly turning, the men stepped to the center of the crumbled stone walls that once made a three-sided structure, its open face looking out over the black gorge.

Squatting down next to a twelve-inch-thick wall block, Dr. Morris spit on his fingers, then rubbed them across the smooth, blackened rock face. Tasting, he looked up, "They're charred—the inside walls of this structure are charred." Standing, he slowly paced the inside edge of the crumbled wall, following it to a waist-high stone block. Reaching out, he gently let his fingers follow the perfectly smooth,

He let his finger gently trace the eight crosses.

hollowed-out bowl in its center. "Look at this workmanship—I've never seen anything constructed with such accuracy and care. It's an exquisite washbasin, most likely used for cleansing after offering to the Lord," he whispered reverently.

"Think this is it, John? Have we got our sacrificial altar?"

"No question it's an altar of sorts, and if it's the one the old chief spoke of . . ." Turning, he raised his arm, pointing toward the black canyon wall looming upward toward the snow line, and in a firm voice said, "then straight up there—that's where the *Muhtar* claims to have seen the Ark!"

For half an hour the men pushed forward, following the ancient stone trail up the side of the canyon. With barely a hundred paces to the snow line, the earth shuddered. As they looked up, a car-sized boulder silently tumbled down the snow slope, shooting huge geysers of ice skyward. "Boulder comin'!" yelled John, as the massive, twisting missile flew overhead, then hit the rocks below in a thunderous roar. For a split second the three men stood stunned, their eyes following the smashing boulder. Suddenly the air filled with whistling rocks spinning like deadly buzz saws. "Rock slide! Run for it!" screamed John as he charged uphill trying to reach the safety of a rock overhang. A fist-sized rock blasted into his backpack, knocking him back down the slope. Twisting to his knees, he tore his backpack off, then in a crouch, dodged, jumped, and rolled as the missiles shot past in hundred-mile-per-hour blurs. Twisting an ankle, he fell flat, covering his head with his arms. Shrapnel-like shards from fracturing rocks whizzed just inches over his prone body. Lying helpless as the stone bullets ricocheted, he shouted, "Lord, I commit myself into Your hands. Help us, Father." Again, a series of smashing rocks, and then as quickly as they began, they ceased, the thunder of the avalanche echoing into the depths of the gorge far below.

Slowly, John uncovered his head, then got to his hands and knees. Shaking his head, he spit blood from his bruised lip. Looking up, he saw Don stumbling down the slope holding his arm, blood oozing between his fingers.

"We've gotta find Brian. Last I saw, he was rolling on down!"

Pulling himself to his feet, John followed, stumbling and sliding down to where they could make out a twisted leg wedged between boulders. Dropping to their knees, the men clawed away rocks covering Brian's back.

"My leg—it's pinned," groaned Brian facedown.

"Come on, Don, put your good shoulder to it!" Both men heaved; the boulder moved slightly. "Once more, Don. This time pull out, Brian." Grunting, the men heaved; Brian yanked hard, rolled over, then sat up, rubbing his bruised leg. "We'd better retrieve what's left of our gear and make for base camp," said John as they hoisted Brian to his feet. Swinging his arms over their shoulders, the three men stumbled through the hot afternoon sun toward base camp and the waiting Ali.

CHAPTER 5

The bright evening campfire reflected off the six weathered faces of the combined expedition teams and the young Kurd at base camp. Further back, flickering shadows danced across the tents and helicopter.

"Man, if this doesn't beat all," said Chuck, shaking his head at the flames. "There we were on the caldera lookin' for avalanches, and what do we get? Terrorists! Here you guys are, down here in the gorge lookin' for terrorists, and what do ya' get? Avalanche!" Looking sideways, he leaned back on an elbow, "Ya' know, John, between our gettin' chased off the caldera and you guys gettin' half-buried alive, well, I've gotta believe there just might be somethin' about those evil spirits our

Commandant and Ali's grandpa, the *Muhtar*, talked about. What'd he call them, Ali?"

"*Djinn*," said Ali, his wide eyes staring at Chuck's big, red, handlebar mustache.

"Yeah, *djinn*. I mean, a man's gotta admit there's somebody or something up there that's doin' its best to stop us. Anyway, John, put on your geologist's hat and tell us what you make of the cave, the stone of eight, and the altar of sacrifice. Sounds like mighty interestin' clues to me."

Reaching over, John poked the fire with his stick, sending sparks into the jet-black night. "Well, the carvings of the turbaned men in robes, carrying staffs and the four-legged animal between them, usually indicate an animal sacrifice. We know the Hittites were a major nation at the time of Abraham, and we also know from the Bible that Abraham lived just a few generations after Noah, having lived not too long after the Flood. If this cave is pre-Hittite, then most likely the carvings were made by direct and very close descendants of Noah. It was probably used at first as a dwelling place, then later as a burial chamber." Throwing a nod across the fire, he said, "Brian even found a huge sarcophagus, or stone coffin, in a side room." Pushing the brim of his leather hat back, then rubbing his chin, he continued, "Now the stone of eight turns out to be a marker with eight distinct Sumerian crosses carved on it. The Sumerians are one of the most ancient civilizations on earth. I gotta believe the marker is a tombstone, or at least a permanent marker of religious significance, and its close proximity to the sacrificial altar is very meaningful. Eight crosses on a tombstone below the altar? Well, guys, think about it—there were eight people on the Ark. And," he poked the fire again with his stick, "there were eight patriarchs who had died before the Flood; some ancient writings suggest their remains had been taken on the Ark. Coincidence? Perhaps, but let's consider the three-walled structure on top of the flat rock above the tombstone."

"Hey! That's the clue in the *Muhtar's* story that seemed to be the most significant to me," said Don.

John nodded agreement and said, "I'm no archaeologist, but as an engineering geologist, I've studied it in some depth and can rule out some speculations. The structure certainly wasn't a lookout tower or fortress because it was too small to contain men for long periods of time. It had no windows and only three walls. I believe, with the evidence of the charred walls and burnt debris on the floor, it was most definitely an altar used for sacrificing large animals."

"Fascinating," said Chuck, throwing another chunk of dried cattle dung on the fire. "Everything you've said fits with the clues the *Muhtar* gave you." Leaning forward, he squinted at John. "But tales from old men are one thing; raw fact, well, that's another. How does all that square with the Bible?"

"Well," said John, settling back on one elbow, "you're absolutely right. Since the Bible is the only book God ever wrote, it is our only source of truth on the subject. Fortunately, in the Book of Genesis there's a record of civilization from Creation through the Flood. Recognize it was only a couple thousand years after God had created everything in six, literal, twenty-four-hour days that man fell away from his Creator and became totally wicked—everyone, that is, except Noah. Now, we know God told Noah He was going to destroy all land-dwelling things that breathed air, except for Noah, his wife, their three sons, their wives, and a very select number of each kind of animal. He said water would cover the entire earth and drown them all." Looking at Ali, he continued, "God instructed Noah to build a huge ship to His exact specifications. That barge could carry forty million pounds inside, had three decks and special rooms for animal stalls and storage. We also know for a fact that He told Noah to cover the Ark inside and out with pitch, making it even more watertight; and that's significant."

"How'd he get all the animals on board?" asked a wide-eyed Ali.

"Yeah, Dr. Morris, how does one catch an eight-hundred-pound gorilla?" chuckled Don from across the flames.

"Very carefully," laughed Chuck with the other men.

"Good question, Ali. But here, look in the Bible at Genesis 6:18-20. It says Noah didn't have to do a thing; God brought all the animals and He got them on the Ark. The animals probably didn't have to go very far since they

lived very close together before the Flood.
Remember, the world was very different
then—no high mountains, no deep oceans,
and only one ocean surrounding one conti-
nent. So there would be plenty of water on
earth for the Flood. In fact, if all the land
smoothed out, the water would cover the
earth to a depth of nearly ten thousand feet."

"What about room for all the animals?"

"Ali's got a good point, John," said B. J. from
the shadows. "There's an awful lot of those
critters out there."

"According to Genesis 7:2, God had two, or
seven, of each kind of land-dwelling, air-breath-
ing animal board the Ark. We don't know how
many kinds there were in Noah's day, but today
there are less than twenty thousand different
kinds. Don't forget, he didn't have to take along
the sea animals. Anyway, we know the Ark
was big enough to hold more than fifty
thousand animals with plenty of room to
spare."

"Anybody ever think about dinosaurs?"
asked Bob. "You know, those dudes are
reptiles, and the older they get, the bigger they
get. I was on a dig one time in Montana when

we uncovered one. Yeow! Was he huge! That monster went up over a couple hundred thousand pounds. Now that's a lot of animal!"

"I suspect dinosaurs were on the Ark, but think about it. Would you have taken along a huge, old, worn-out monster? Logic tells you smaller, younger, sturdier stock would be best. Anyway, we know they survived the Flood and grew 'cause Job, who lived after the Flood, talks of seeing 'behemoth' that had a tail as big as a giant tree, and 'leviathan' that breathed out fire and smoke."

"Sounds like a dragon to me," called Brian, moving his sore leg closer to the fire's warmth.

"My grandpa *Muhtar* has many ancient stories of such beasts roaming the marshes of the foothills in times past."

"Exactly, Ali, and no doubt that's where the dragon stories come from. You know, every culture on earth talks of a world-covering flood. The Bible says in Genesis 7 that it rained for forty days and forty nights, and the great underground fountains of the deep were opened up. Water covered the face of the entire earth. We know scientifically this is absolutely true, because even the highest mountaintops have fossils of ocean animals buried in the rocks." Tapping the volcanic rocks that ringed the fire pit with his stick, John went on, "Even these stones speak to that truth. They're what we geologists call pillow lava—that's lava that's been ejected from *under* deep ocean water; and here we are, eight thousand feet *above* sea level! No question about it," he nodded back toward the black, looming peak, "at one time, that entire mountain was most definitely under water. And when the mountain rose and the water receded—," pausing, he raised the tip of his burning stick toward the mountaintop, "well, right up there is where we believe God says the Ark landed. The Bible says it landed on the 'mountains of Ararat,' and this is the only significant mountain in this ancient country called 'Ararat.' And the very first thing Noah did after getting everyone off the Ark was to build an altar and make burnt offerings to God."

"I can understand how you guys may have found Noah's sacrificial altar—it's made outta stone. But if the Ark is periodically exposed to air, well, how could it still be preserved today? I mean, the Bible says God told Noah to make it out of wood—wouldn't it have rotted by now? It's been sittin' up there almost five thousand years."

"Good point, B. J., but remember God also told Noah to cover both the inside and outside of the Ark with pitch. That's a tarlike substance which most likely would've preserved the barge, especially if it'd been trapped in ice or snow for most of the time. It's also possible that it was buried by volcanic ash during a later eruption and has petrified—turned to solid rock. We'll never know till we actually find it."

"Talk about the Ark being trapped in snow and ice, now that's my specialty," said Chuck, sitting up. "Here, pass these drawings around. They were made by various people who claimed to have seen a portion of the Ark after the sun had melted the ice back. Look there, that first one was drawn by a shepherd boy just like Ali back in 1905. He stumbled on it while looking for his goats. Here's the second one made by some Russian soldiers who climbed the mountain back in 1917. Now, look at these sketches made by two different pilots flying over the mountain, one during World

War II and the other as recently as 1974. Notice, every one of those drawings has the same basic picture—the front of the Ark is poking out, snow drifted over the center, and the rear of the boat is trapped deep under ice, all on the edge of a steep cliff. Now, hang on to your hats, guys, 'cause on our way around the mountain today, just as we were coming in at sunset, the clouds parted; and we got one fleeting glance at that ice ledge up there," he said, pointing up the black mountain. "And what you see in those crude sketches is exactly what all three of us saw. We tried to swing around, but by then the clouds had closed in again. We couldn't have landed anyway 'cause it's above the hovering capability of the chopper, and we had no place to skid in like we did up on the caldera. But we saw it for sure. Right, guys?"

"He's absolutely right," said B. J., looking at Bob.

"Matter of fact, I even got videos of it!"

The stunned climbers sat transfixed as they watched the video footage on the camera's internal monitor. Dr. Morris sat upright in thoughtful silence, his eyes scanning the mountain's blackness, then fixing on each man individually. The flames reflected the excited anticipation on their ruddy faces. "You up for it, Brian? The leg okay?"

"Absolutely."

"How about the arm, Don?"

"Count me in."

"Your team, Chuck?"

"You couldn't keep us off that mountain, *djinn* or no *djinn*. We're with you, Big John."

"Then, that settles it. First light, we mount the final assault!"

ᛞ   ᛞ   ᛞ

As the men reached the steepest part of the upper canyon wall, snow began to fall. John yelled over the rising wind to the team, "Brian, you, B. J., and I will make the final assault. Chuck, you, Don, and Bob make a support station down here. Should we need help or spot the Ark, I'll send up a flare." Pointing up the slope, he yelled sideways, "We'll rope up across that finger glacier, then make for that rocky protrusion toward the crest. We should get a good view of the entire area from up there." With a quick "thumbs up," the assault team stepped off into the snowfall. For an hour the three men groped across the glacier as the temperature dropped and the wind howled. Snow began to come in torrents. A bright flash and thunder exploded upward from a boulder twenty paces away. Lightning flashed again as dense clouds enveloped the trio. Huge amounts of static electricity were collecting on the larger rocks, then exploding outward in deafening thunderclaps. They were in the very center of an electrical storm. From the journal of Dr. Morris, he later recounted:

> Static electricity was building everywhere. Our ice axes and crampons were singing, our hair stood on end, even B. J.'s beard and my mustache stood straight out. We could actually feel the electricity build on our bodies. Staggering forward, I glanced back and saw Brian and B. J. collapse beneath a large boulder. I had seen lightning hit that very boulder just seconds before. Through the blinding snow and exploding electrical bolts, I stumbled back toward them to warn of certain catastrophe. Too late—just as I slid and stumbled down to them, a slashing bolt hit the rock again, sending unbelievable jolts of electricity through all three of us. B. J. was

frozen to the rock by his back; his arms, legs, and head stood out stiffly; his whole body surged with electricity. Brian and I were instantly catapulted up and out. The force of the lightning seemed to suspend us in midair, then dropped us far down the slope. Back at the rock, B. J., shaking violently, forced one leg to the ground, thereby completing an electrical circuit which blasted him into the air. Landing nearby, he somersaulted past us in a geyser of ice and snow.

Rolling over on my hands and knees, I managed to rise to a crouch. Another bolt struck me, catapulting me up spread-eagle. The expected landing impact never came—it seems I floated for several seconds, then was gently laid down as if by unseen hands. My whole body went numb, but I never lost consciousness. Slowly at first, I started to slide down the slope, then faster and faster; snow gouged my face as I slid; my body bounced off rocks. I had to stop. I tried reaching for the rocks, but my arms were like jelly. It was a total, living nightmare.

Then, crunch! I wedged between boulders. For a few seconds, I lay there in intense pain. Trying to roll over, I discovered my legs were paralyzed. Grabbing them, there was no sensation of touch, only burning, searing pain. Over the roaring wind and snow, I called for help. A muffled reply came from up the hill.

Twisting, I squinted into the screaming storm and caught the blurry sight of B. J. sitting, his arms limp, one leg pinned under him. "I'm paralyzed," he called, his head slumped to his chest. Hearing a moan down below, I twisted again. Brian lay facedown ten paces away. One side of his head was white with snow, the other red with blood.

Slowly, Brian got on all fours, then stood, head hanging. We called to him from above as he stumbled up and fell at my feet. Looking up, his eyes were filled with confusion and fear. "Where are we? . . . What's goin' on? . . . What are we doin' here?" In desperation, I shouted, "We're on Mount Ararat. Been hit by lightning." He just looked past me with a blank, bewildered expression, dark red blood running down his head, dripping on the white snow.

Our situation was critical. B. J. and I were paralyzed; Brian was senseless; the storm was gaining in intensity; lightning was slashing everywhere—and we were slowly freezing. As I slumped there contemplating death, Jesus began to interject His thoughts into my mind. I was reminded of the thousands of Christians who had suffered and died while following the Lord's leading, how they considered it a privilege to suffer for Him. I was reminded of the hundreds of Christians praying for us back in America. I was reminded of the job we had been called to do by our Living God, and the vast importance of our mission. Then, somehow I knew God wasn't going to let us die in that frozen wasteland; and if I had that faith, the faith that God gave me when I accepted Jesus as my personal Savior, then I could pray that prayer of faith, knowing He would hear me. Putting my head back, I called into the teeth of the raging wind, "Lord, breathe life into this body!"

As Brian once more got to his feet and stood weaving in front of me, I tried to move my legs—no response. Once more I tried—nothing. Then my fingers flexed— then my arms tingled and moved. Frantically, I beat my legs with clubbed hands. Gradually, feeling came to my hands; and as I massaged my numb legs, little by little I sensed the firmness return to them. At first

they felt like balloons filled with water—
senseless and pliable. Looking up, I saw
Brian again drop to all fours, head hanging.
Time was of the essence. Again massaging
vigorously, I threw snow on my legs to
ease the burning sensation. Rolling to my
side, then to my knees, I pushed up, literally leaning into the wind, using it as a
crutch. Stumbling, I fell beside B. J. and
pulled his pinned leg out from under him.
As I beat and massaged the paralyzed flesh,
another bolt exploded a few feet away,
showering us with ice chunks. B. J. looked
calm and relaxed. Nodding, he shouted for
me to help Brian, who had managed to
crawl on all fours beneath another large rock.
Crawling across the snow, I grabbed a parka
off his discarded backpack and wrapped it
around his violently shaking body. As I
pulled the drawstring tight, our eyes met.
Through frozen lids, a glimmer of recogni-
tion crossed his face. "What's goin' on, John?
Where's B. J.?" He grabbed my shoulders,
shook his head, then genuine concern and
rational thought came back to him. Thank
God!

Brian got up and helped me drag B. J.
back to a cliff face, which gave us only a

slight relief from the gale. We desperately needed a flat place to pitch a tent and gain some degree of shelter from the raging storm. Our only hope was on top of the rock ridge a hundred yards higher up the slope. Brian and I followed a trail of boulders up the near-vertical slope to the ridge crest. Once reaching it, we fell flat as the wind velocity on top nearly doubled. Still, this area was our only hope of clearing the lightning bolts and pitching a tent. We tumbled back down to B. J. He was massaging his legs—the right had regained strength, but nothing in the left. He still couldn't stand, so Brian and I once more climbed the slope with all three packs. We drove anchors in the ice and dropped a rope to assist us in our effort to get B. J. up. My legs started to shake like Jell-O; both of us collapsed, totally exhausted. "We've got to make it. He'll freeze down there," I shouted into Brian's ear over the howling wind. Once more we crawled and stumbled on all fours down the slope. To our amazement, B. J. was upright; his legs still had no feeling, yet their strength had returned enough to allow him to stand one more time. The three of us stumbled, clawed, and crawled back up the slope through the bolts that exploded on both sides of us. Pushing from beneath while Brian pulled from above, we gave one last mighty heave, clearing the ridge. Crawling up, all three of us collapsed, gasping for precious oxygen. Lying face up with my legs numb, my back pain-wracked, my arms shaking violently, I thought this was the end. Just before I closed my eyes for what seemed like the last time, I saw it—or at least thought I did. Was it real? Yes, there it was again. For a fleeting second, a patch of blue sky, then another. Then, just as suddenly as it had started, the storm broke. Watching the last puffy clouds disappear, leaving a pure blue sky, and feeling the howling wind subside to a whisper, I knew our trial was over. I guess the Lord figured we had had enough and simply answered our prayers. As the three of us lay there absorbing the sun's healing warmth, nobody spoke; yet we all felt the same thing—His grace was sufficient, we would make it.

ও ও ও

At base camp, the combined American teams and the young Kurdish lad paused after breaking camp in preparation for the helicopter shuttle off the mountain. They stood silently in a semicircle looking one last time at the upper reaches of the black gorge, now completely white under ten feet of fresh snow. In the center stood Ali, his eyes misting. Hesitantly, he reached up and took the hand of the big American standing next to him, "*Muhtar* will say that *Gemi* is once again hidden in mystery. I think, Dr. John, it will be a very great miracle when one day you find the Ark." Squeezing the lad's hand, John said quietly, "I believe we were close, Ali, mighty close. Now we'll just have to wait for another season when once again the sun melts back the ice and snow." Looking down into the lad's sad eyes, he continued, "But finding the Ark is not the *real* miracle, Ali."

"Then what is the real miracle, Dr. John?" said Ali looking at the American.

"Well," said Dr. Morris as he dropped to one knee, pushed the brim of his hat back, and put his arm around the boy's slender shoulder. "Remember when I first met you and was torn with mountain sickness, and you, Ali, went and took your prized lamb and killed him especially for me. I know that made you very, very sad to have to sacrifice that special lamb." The young boy nodded, his chin dropping to his chest. "But then the next morning when you saw I was cured and strong again by eating your lamb, well, you were very, very happy." Lifting the boy's chin with his finger, "Big John" said softly, "Right, Ali?" The small Kurdish boy nodded and smiled bravely despite tears flowing down his cheeks. "Well, Ali, the Living God did the same thing for me and you."

"He did?"

"Yes. You see, Ali, many seasons after the Flood all men again disobeyed God and became sick with sin in their hearts. So God sent His only Son to earth as a baby. He was born from a virgin. He called His Son the Lamb of God. His earthly mother named Him Jesus. Then when He was grown, God permitted wicked men to crucify Jesus on a cross. God sacrificed His Son, His Lamb, to provide a way for all mankind to be healed of their sickness of sin. The Bible, written by the power of God, says, 'whoever believes in Him [Jesus] should not perish but have everlasting life.' That is the free gift of salvation. There is nothing you can do to earn it; all you have to do is accept it. And when this happens, it makes God very, very happy."

"How do I accept this gift of God's Lamb?"

"Simply confess to Jesus that you are a sinner, say you are sorry for your sins, and ask Jesus into your heart. Then He promises to make you a new person. Jesus calls that being 'born again.' And that, Ali, is the real miracle!"

Brightening, the lad turned and looked at John, "Then I, Ali, will ask Jesus into my heart; and when you come back to once again search for the hidden Ark, I shall be here waiting for you as a new person." Squaring his shoulders under his tattered shirt, he looked from man to man. "And perhaps you American men will allow me, Ali, future *Muhtar*, to become one of your team and search for the lost Ark. This time, up there," he said twisting and pointing his slender arm toward the huge, majestic mountain showing brilliant white against the pure blue sky.

Kneeling, Chuck put his arm around the boy's other shoulder and said, "Ali, I know God will be honored to have a brave lad like you on His team, and so will we!"

EPILOGUE

D r. John Morris holds a bachelor of science degree in civil engineering from Virginia Tech. He received his master of science and doctorate in geological engineering from the University of Oklahoma in 1977 and 1980, respectively. He has received a Phillips Petroleum Graduate Fellowship and the Sun Oil Teaching Award. John has written and coauthored a number of books and publications, including *Noah's Ark and the Ararat Adventure* and *The Young Earth.*

John is currently President and professor of geology at the Institute for Creation Research. He has traveled much of the world on field expeditions, researching, and documenting scientific creationism, including thirteen expeditions to Mount Ararat. Most recently, he has returned from Russia where, among other duties, he gave a symposium to the Russian Science Academy on science and creation.

Dr. Morris and his wife Dalta and their three children live in Santee, California.

න න න

Chuck Aaron is vice president of Tsirah Corporation. As an adventurer/explorer, he has made six expeditions to Mount Ararat in Turkey. With his fifteen thousand hours of flight time in a helicopter, Chuck is the only American pilot approved to fly in restricted Turkish airspace along the borders of Russia, Iran, and Iraq.

Chuck resides in West Chicago, Illinois, with his wife Linda and their three children.

ABOUT THE AUTHOR

P aul Thomsen graduated from the University of Wisconsin (Madison) in 1960. Through his career as an international executive and corporate owner, he has lived in and traveled much of the world.

Paul and his wife, Julie, have created Dynamic Genesis, Inc. and endeavor to produce books for the Creation Adventure Series of which *Mystery of the Ark* is a part. They also conduct seminars for school students, teaching them to answer questions on origins the way the public school textbooks present them, and then "qualify" their answers with a nongradable, biblical, scientific answer. This "qualifier" system has received enthusiastic approval from both teachers and students.

The Thomsens have seven children and live on a small lake in northern Wisconsin.